Tales of the Riverbank

Riverbank Regatta and other stories

DAVE ELLISON

Illustrated by

PAULINE HAZELWOOD

Hippo

Scholastic Children's Books,
Scholastic Publications Ltd,
7-9 Pratt Street, London NW1 OAE

Scholastic Inc.,
730 Broadway, New York, NY 10003, USA

Scholastic Canada Ltd,
123 Newkirk Road, Richmond Hill,
Ontario, Canada L4C 3G5

Ashton Scholastic Pty Ltd,
PO Box 579, Gosford, New South Wales,
Australia

Ashton Scholastic Ltd,
Private Bag 1, Penrose, Auckland,
New Zealand

First published in the UK by Scholastic Publications Limited, 1993

Text copyright © by Dave Ellison, 1993
Illustration copyright © by Pauline Hazelwood, 1993
Based on the TV series created by Dave Ellison and Paul Sutherland

ISBN: 0 590 55420 4
Printed in Belgium by Proost Book Production

CONTENTS

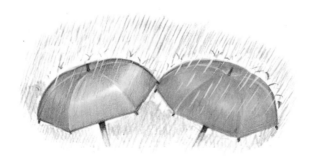

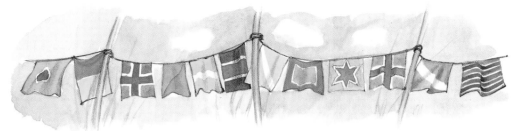

RIVERBANK REGATTA

The riverbank regatta was the big event of the year, and nearly everybody took part. Roderick Rat, of course, would enter his motor boat and as today was the day before the race, he was busy making sure that everything was in working order.

"Now, let's see," he muttered to himself. "I've checked the oil, filled up with petrol, changed the spark plug; now all I've got to do is polish the paint." Which is exactly what he did.

Mr Gerbil was hard at work at his boatyard, selling anything that would float to a crowd of customers, all of whom wanted to enter the race.

"No, of course the canoe won't sink," he said to Spiky Hedgehog. "It's made of best quality birch bark."

"Emmm... I don't know," replied Spiky. "These sides look awful thin."

"Gerry... Gerry... I want a mast," called a voice from the crowd.

"Yes, and I want some sails," shouted another.

Mr Gerbil was indeed busy.

The start of the race was going to be signalled by the firing of the riverbank canon, and Hammy had been given the important job of setting it off.

"Hmmm… I *think* I know how to do it," he muttered as he read the instructions. "All I have to do is light the fuse and stand back."

"And even a hamster can do that," said Frog, who happened to be passing.

Now, Guinea Pig wasn't too keen to enter the race, mainly because he didn't have a boat. But as all his friends were taking part, he decided to take a nice hot bath and think it over. "I could get a boat from Mr Gerbil," he said, as he splashed himself with a sponge. "Trouble is, all his boats seem to sink." Then, with a mass of bubbles floating around his head, he put his great brain to work. He thought… and he thought… and then he thought some more - and then, when you would think that he had no more thought left to think, he suddenly stood up, blew all the bubbles away and shouted, "I've got it! I'll race the race in my bath." And so saying, he pulled out the plug and all the water drained away.

The morning of the regatta started bright and early. Boats of every type and size were crowding the water, and excitement was high as everyone prepared for the start.

"You can't enter the race in a bath," shouted Roderick from his motor boat as GP launched his tub into the water.

"Why not?" replied Guinea Pig. "It's got a mast and a sail." And so it had. GP had used a broom handle as a mast and an old sheet as a sail and, as far as he was concerned, he was ready for the race to begin.

"Are you ready…?" shouted the hamster. Then, without waiting for a reply, he lit the fuse. A bright sparkle made its way along the wire, fizzing and hissing its way up to the cannon. Then, as it reached the great gun, it disappeared down the barrel. With a loud *Bang!* and a great cloud of smoke, the race began.

Now, unfortunately, no-one had issued any rules and no-one knew which way to go. Roderick headed off upstream, because that was the way he was pointing, and all the other boats which had motors followed him, thinking he knew the way. But they were wrong.

All the boats with sails, however, went the other way because that was the way the wind was taking them. Mr Hedgehog, who hadn't got a motor or a sail on his canoe, didn't move at all - which was just as well, because his spiky coat had made a mass of holes in the side of the boat and he was sinking.

Meanwhile, Guinea Pig sat grandly in his bath boat and let the wind push him slowly along… backwards. Mr Frog had entered on a lily pad and was busy going round in circles and Mr Turtle, who had fixed a mast and sail to the top of his shell, was going along quite well - that is, until he went to sleep and sank to the bottom of the river.

That left GP who, by now, was quite close to the finishing line.

"Yippee!" he cried. "I'm going to be the first across the line!"

Then, in his excitement, he pulled out the plug and the bath boat sank.

"Oh dear," he spluttered, as he swam ashore, "I always pull the plug out when I've finished with the bath."

Poor Guinea Pig, he hadn't won the race after all. But then he hadn't lost the race either, because no-one had won, and if no-one had won, then no-one had lost, and if you haven't lost, you must have won.

Oh, dear, regattas are very confusing.

SLOW BUT SURE

Mr Turtle was the riverbank postman. He had been the postman for as long as anyone could remember, and everyone gave him a cheery wave as he made his way from one bright red letter box to another, collecting the mail.

"Slow but sure," he muttered to himself as he carefully put a letter into the large bag that was tied to his back. "Slow but sure, that's what I always say."

Back home, at his post office, Turtle would sort the mail out. Huge piles of parcels and great stacks of letters were everywhere about.

"This one goes to Roderick…This one goes to Mr Badger…This one goes to… oh, that one goes to me." On he went, sorting the mail, slowly and very surely. But not everyone was sure about the *surely*.

"Oh dear, oh dear," muttered Miss Much to herself, "this letter has taken ages to get here. It's an invitation to Mr Hedgehog's Christmas party…last year!"

It was much the same at Hammy Hamster's old boot house. "Oh my," he said excitedly as he opened his front door. "The postman has left a parcel on my doorstep."

Now the hamster had never received a parcel before, so it took him quite a time to open it. Finally, when the last piece of string was untied and the last sheet of brown paper torn apart, he stood back in amazement.

"A Christmas pudding? But it's the middle of summer. This must be the parcel Roderick said he sent to me at the end of last year."

Poor Turtle, he may be sure but he certainly is slow. So slow that Gerry Gerbil, the second-hand boat dealer, was very worried. "I sent out those bills weeks ago," he said to his secretary, Miss Mouse, "and no-one has paid me anything yet."

"They all say they didn't get the bills," replied Miss Mouse. "Are you sure you posted them?"

"That's what it is, it's the post. It's that Turtle," went on the gerbil. "He's much too slow. He'll just have to go."

Then, after a moment's pause, he went on, "What's needed is someone with fast transport to take the mail along the river."

Miss Mouse fluttered her long eyelashes and smiled at Gerry Gerbil. "I think I know the very person," she said.

"You do?" asked the gerbil. "Who?"

"Why, you," replied Miss Mouse.

"Of course," said the gerbil. "I'll be the postman! I'll deliver the mail by boat."

13

Now, Guinea Pig and Roderick knew nothing about Gerry Gerbil's idea. But they did know about Mr Turtle's slow delivery of the mail.

"What's needed is someone who can get from one end of the river to the other quickly," said Roderick. "Someone like Mr Owl. He can fly very quickly."

"No," replied GP. "He'd never get off the ground. The mail bags would be much too heavy. Anyway, he only flies at night, and who would want the mail delivered at night?"

So the two friends started to think. First they thought of this, then they thought of that. Then, just before lunchtime, Guinea Pig's great brain suddenly thought of the answer.

"I will be the postman," announced GP. "I will deliver the post by air."

"But you can't fly," said the rat.

"No," replied the guinea pig, "but my aeroplane can."

"Oh no," said Roderick, "not your aeroplane!"

Later that afternoon, just as Hammy was eating a slice of Christmas pudding, he had a visitor. It was Mr Guinea Pig. "Come on, Hammy, I need some help." With a gulp, Hammy finished his Christmas pudding and the two friends set off.

"Where are we going?" asked Hammy as they ran along, side by side.

"We're going to my hangar," puffed GP.

"Oh my," said Hammy. "Oh my, oh my." Then, after quite a bit more running, he asked, "What's a hangar?"

"That's a hangar," said GP as they arrived at the edge of the grassy meadow. "That over there." He pointed across to a large wooden building.

"Looks like a shed to me," said Hammy.

"No," replied the guinea pig. "When a shed has got an aeroplane inside, it is called a hangar."

"Oh, I see," said Hammy and then, with a puzzled look on his face, he asked, "What's an aeroplane?"

Guinea Pig unlocked a large padlock and swung back the heavy wooden doors.

"*That's* an aeroplane," said GP. Standing in front of them, covered in cobwebs and dust, was Guinea Pig's wonderful flying machine.

"Oh my," said Hammy. "Oh my, oh my."

Which, under the circumstances, was all that needed to be said.

Back at Gerry Gerbil's boatyard, things were getting busy. Gerry had painted his fastest boat bright red, oiled the engine, polished the brass and was now busy screwing a smart wooden sign onto the bow which announced in bold black letters, *Post boat*.

"Poor Turtle," said Gerry to Miss Mouse. "He'll be out of a job when I start my fast delivery service."

Miss Mouse fluttered her long eyelashes, smiled at the gerbil and said, "That's progress."

Progress was certainly being made back at GP's hangar. The two friends had pushed the aeroplane out onto the grass, dusted it down, and painted it bright red. Now, they were tying a large flag to a mast they had fixed just behind the cockpit. On the flag was written, *Post plane*.

"Poor Turtle," said Hammy. "He'll be out of a job when you start your fast delivery service."

Guinea Pig stared proudly at his aeroplane and said, "That's progress."

Next morning, as is usual along the riverbank, all the animals except, of course, for Mr Owl, were up and about bright and early. Every one of them was busily being busy. Gerry Gerbil and Mr Guinea Pig were the busiest of them all.

"That's it," said Gerry as he stuffed one last letter into an already overflowing mail bag. "Turtle couldn't have collected this much mail in all his life."

And he was probably quite right, for he was surrounded by bags of all shapes and sizes, each one filled to the brim with mail.

Further along the river the guinea pig was doing much the same thing, except that he was putting all the letters and parcels into two boxes he had fixed to the wings of his aeroplane."That's it," he said as the last of the mail was loaded. "Stand by for take-off!"

Quickly, he climbed into the cockpit and pushed the starter. With a roar and several puffs of black smoke, the engine started and Guinea Pig's post plane took off. The mail was on its way.

Meanwhile, Gerry Gerbil was also on his way. With all the mailbags piled into his boat, he was speeding along the river, eager to make his first delivery.

"Make way!" he shouted out. "Make way for the mail!"

"Quack… quack… Not so fast," complained Mrs Duck. "You'll wake Mr Turtle."

Now Mr Turtle had been rather puzzled. He hadn't found any mail to deliver that morning at all.

"Maybe I'll have an extra big load tomorrow," he thought. Then he slowly made his way to his favourite spot along the river, snuggled into his shell and went to sleep.

It was just after Gerry Gerbil had passed the sleeping turtle that GP arrived high over the home of Roderick Rat. "Ah, I've got a parcel for Roderick...Where is it?" He leaned out of the cockpit and rummaged around in the box.

Gerbil, who had also got some mail for Roderick, heard GP's aeroplane buzzing around and was amazed to see what was written on the aeroplane's flag.

"You can't deliver mail by air!" he shouted up to Guinea Pig. "I'm delivering the mail by boat."

But GP didn't hear a word. He'd got a problem. "It's stuck. Roderick's parcel is stuck..." The guinea pig was struggling to free the parcel, the aeroplane was twisting and turning, and then, with a loud *twang!* the strap holding the box onto the wing snapped.

"Oh, no!" cried GP. "It's slipping… I can't hold it!" And then it was gone.

Gerry had almost arrived at Roderick's house to make his delivery when he heard a loud *whoosh*… followed by a *thump* and a *crunch* - and suddenly he was all wet.

"Help! Help! I'm sinking!" he cried. Then, without one more thought about delivering the mail, he swam to the shore.

Guinea Pig's mail box had fallen directly onto Gerry Gerbil's post boat, smashed right through the deck and made a hole in the bottom. The post boat and all the mail sank beneath the water.

For the next few days, Mr Turtle was busy, very busy. All day long he swam down to the bottom of the river searching for the mail. One by one he found each letter and every parcel, and took them to the surface to dry. Then, with his old mail bag tied to his back and all the letters and parcels safely tied up inside, he set out to make his delivery.

"Slow but sure," he muttered to himself. "Slow but sure, that's what I always say."

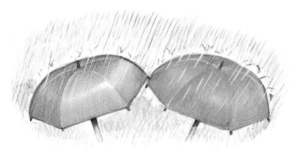

THE FLOOD

It was raining. It had been raining the day before, and it had been raining the day before that. In fact, it had been raining for five whole days. Everywhere and everything was wet. Very wet. It had rained for so long that the river had filled to the very edge of its banks and the water had spilled across the fields and meadows and into the mysterious wood, flooding the homes of all who lived along it.

Poor Roderick, who lived right on the river bank, was sitting in his boat sheltering under a large umbrella sadly watching the water as it made its way under his front door and into his home.

"Oh dear…" he muttered to himself, "everything will be ruined."

Further along the river, Mr Frog was also having problems. The water had risen so high that his lily pad home was now below the surface and he was sitting in the only dry place he could find.

"Hurrumph… Whoever heard of a frog sitting in a tree?" he grumbled to anyone who cared to listen.

"Whoever heard of a *rabbit* sitting in a tree?" replied a voice from a branch further up.

"No-one," said the frog and then, looking up, he saw that he was not alone. Mr Rabbit, Mrs Rabbit and all their little rabbits were sitting, wet and shivering, on the branch above.

"I'm hungry…" said a baby rabbit.

"I want to go home…" said another.

But the water continued to swirl beneath them and there was nothing they could do.

All around the riverbank the animals' homes were flooded and all that they could do was climb onto their roofs or up to the tops of their chimneys and wait to be rescued.

Now, Hammy was lucky. His old boot house had been built on top of a hill and was quite dry.

"Oh my, oh my," he said to himself as he looked out from his sitting-room window. "I wish I could do something to help."

At that very moment a large anchor, connected to a long rope, swung into view, crossed his front garden and hooked itself onto a rose bush.

"Come on, Hammy," called a voice from the other end of the rope. "We've got to help!"

Hammy ran outside, looked up the rope, and discovered the guinea pig looking down at him from the basket of his wonderful balloon.

"Everybody is stranded down by the river," he called. "Come on, we'll rescue them in my balloon."

"Oh my," said Hammy as he climbed up the rope. "I've never rescued anyone in all my life."

GP hauled up the anchor and the balloon speedily made its way towards the river.

The first person they came to was Miss Much, who was floating around in an empty tea chest outside her half-submerged shop.

"Oh, thank goodness you've arrived!" she cried out as the guinea pig brought the balloon down, and she climbed into the basket. "I don't know what would have become of me," she sobbed. "I'm so wet and cold and hungry."

The hamster wrapped her in a warm blanket and away they went, searching all the time for someone else to rescue.

"Over there - look!" shouted Hammy. "It's Miss Mouse and Gerry Gerbil." Looking down, GP saw that the two frightened animals had climbed up the mast of a sunken boat in the flooded remains of Gerry's boatyard. In no time at all, they also were safely in the basket which, by now, was rather full.

"We'd better take them back to your boot house," said GP.

"That's a good idea," replied Hammy. "I can make them all a nice cup of tea."

All afternoon, the guinea pig and the hamster flew backwards and forwards along the riverbank rescuing everyone who wanted to be rescued.

"No…not me…" said Turtle, as he drifted along in the water. "I'm quite enjoying this."

Mr Rabbit wasn't enjoying
it, nor was Mrs Rabbit and all
the little rabbits. But they were
soon found by Hammy and
GP, and so was Mr Frog, Spiky
Hedgehog, Bobby Badger and
then, just before the sun set
itself behind the trees, they
found Roderick drifting along

in his waterlogged boat, sadly looking up at them from under his large
umbrella.

"Tea…" he said."That's all I want…a cup of tea."

And, of course, as soon as they got back to the old boot house, that's
exactly what they had.

AN EXTRA SPECIAL DAY

The guinea pig was up bright and early. He had his breakfast, brushed his coat, preened his whiskers, and he was ready.

"Yes," he muttered to himself, "I'm ready." And with that, he hurried out of the old mill, jumped into his jeep and drove off.

Today was an extra special day, and GP was ready to enjoy every moment.

TO THE SHOP

Now, it so happened that all along the riverbank everybody was getting up early. It seemed that they all had something special to do. Miss Much always got up early because she had to open the general store. But this morning she had opened up extra early, and within minutes the whole shop was buzzing with activity. Everyone from one end of the river to the other had come to do some shopping.

"I'll have four sheets of wrapping paper and a large ball of string," said Roderick Rat.

"Oh, yes, I'll have some wrapping paper as well," said Miss Mouse.

"Save some for me…" said a small voice from the crowd.

"And some for me…" called out Hammy, who had just arrived and was busy pushing his way towards the counter.

Miss Much had never seen so many customers in her shop before, and it wasn't long before she had sold all her wrapping paper, all her string, all her blue ribbon, biscuits, cards and buns. She even sold a pile of empty boxes, eight packets of candles, three large boxes of greeting cards, all her paper chains and a large pot of glue.

"Goodness me," she said as she watched the last of her customers struggle away from the shop laden with things that they had bought. "Today is indeed a special day."

Toot, toot, went the jeep as Guinea Pig drove up to Hammy's boot house.

"Hello, Hammy," he called. "You doing anything special today?"

"No," replied the hamster as he came to his front door. "Just packing a few things in an old cardboard box... Nothing special..."

"Oh, I see," said GP.

"Don't you know what day it is?"

"Why, yes, of course," said Hammy. "It's Wednesday... all day long."

"No, that's not what I mean," grumbled Guinea Pig. Then with a rather sad look on his face, he started up his jeep and drove off.

Roderick had been doing something special all morning, but now he was finished. He had just decided to have a little nap in his front garden when the surrounding peace and quiet was shattered by a grinding of gears, two loud bangs and an even louder Toot, toot, from GP's jeep.

"I thought you would be doing something special today," shouted Guinea Pig as the jeep skidded to a halt in a cloud of dust.

"Something special?" replied Roderick. "No, I've nothing special to do. I thought I'd take a little nap." And with that, he closed his eyes, curled up in his deck chair and went to sleep.

"But Roddy," said GP. "Today is…" But it was no good. Roderick was sound asleep.

Poor Guinea Pig's face filled with gloom. Even Roderick, his best friend, had forgotten that today was a rather special day.

And that's how it was all along the river bank. Everywhere he went, everyone he spoke to gave him the same answer. Even old Mr Frog, who knew about everything, didn't know about today.

"No, Mr Guinea Pig, I can't think what's so special about today," he grunted. Then, with a loud *plop!* he jumped into the river and disappeared.

Poor Guinea Pig just couldn't believe it. "No-one has remembered," he said to himself. "Not one of my friends has remembered my special day."

Sadly, he decided to go home. As the afternoon sun shone across the countryside, the sound of GP's jeep could be heard making its way slowly past the mysterious wood, past the empty lily pad patch of old Mr Frog, and past the deserted branch of the wise old owl.

No-one was about. No-one to give a cheery wave. "No-one remembered..." said GP sadly to himself. "No-one remembered."

If anyone had been sitting next to poor Guinea Pig, they would have seen a small tear in the corner of his eye. "What's the point of a day being special if no-one remembers...?" he muttered to himself as he drove up the drive to his old mill.

Sadly, he parked his jeep, climbed out of the driving seat and made his way to the front door. Just as he was about to turn the handle, the old door creaked open and a great shout of "Happy Birthday!" filled the air.

There, gathered in front of him, filling every nook and cranny of his sitting-room, were all his friends. "Happy birthday, GP," they all shouted. "Come on in and have your party!"

For a minute Guinea Pig couldn't think of a word to say. With a big smile, he looked around the room. In the middle was a large birthday cake covered in candles and piled high in one corner were all his presents tied up in blue ribbon.

"I thought you'd forgotten," he said.

"Forgotten?" said Roderick, as he handed him a neatly wrapped box. "How could we forget such an extra special day?"

And, of course, he was right.